Clara and the Binky Fairy

By Donna Miller

Illustrated by Michael Suorsa

Do Rae Mi Publishing

Do Rae Mi Publishing
www.doraemipublishing.net

For information regarding permission, please write to:
Donna Miller
540 Fairview Ave. #25
Arcadia, CA 91007
(626) 251-0365
email: doraemi46@yahoo.com

ISBN 978-0-9823524-1-0
Printed in the United States
First printing, November 2009
Designed by Michael Suorsa

For Clara, who gladly shares her tea cakes with the Monkey Prince and long ago donated her pacifier to the Binky Fairy.

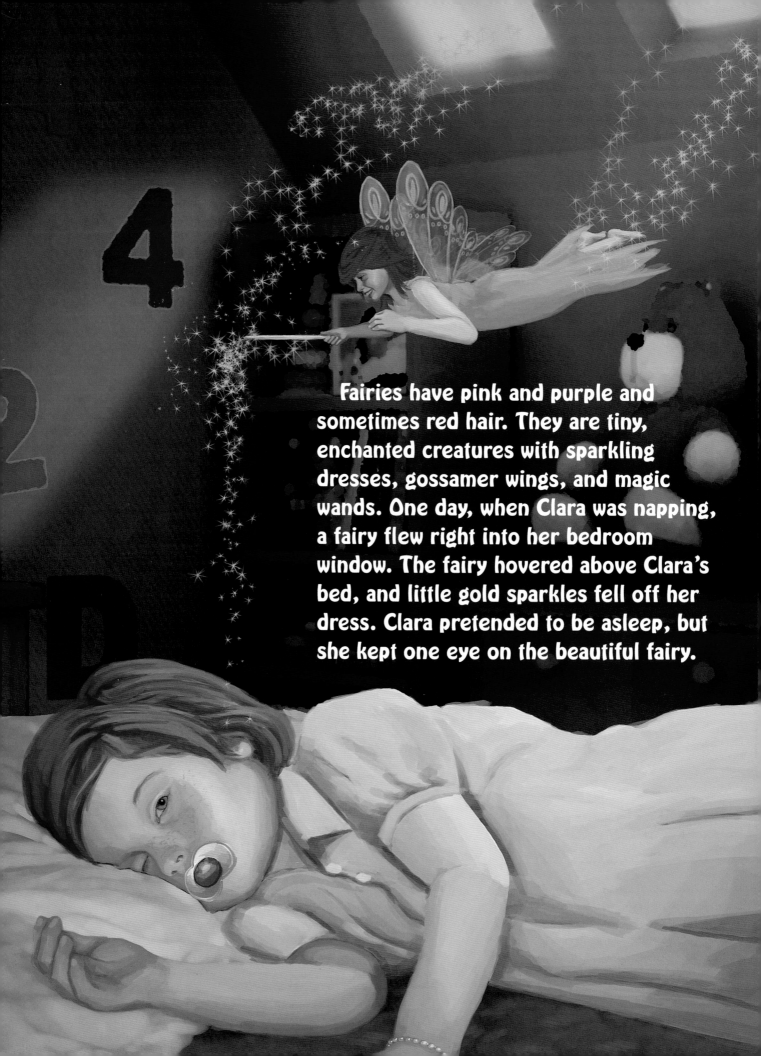

Fairies have pink and purple and sometimes red hair. They are tiny, enchanted creatures with sparkling dresses, gossamer wings, and magic wands. One day, when Clara was napping, a fairy flew right into her bedroom window. The fairy hovered above Clara's bed, and little gold sparkles fell off her dress. Clara pretended to be asleep, but she kept one eye on the beautiful fairy.

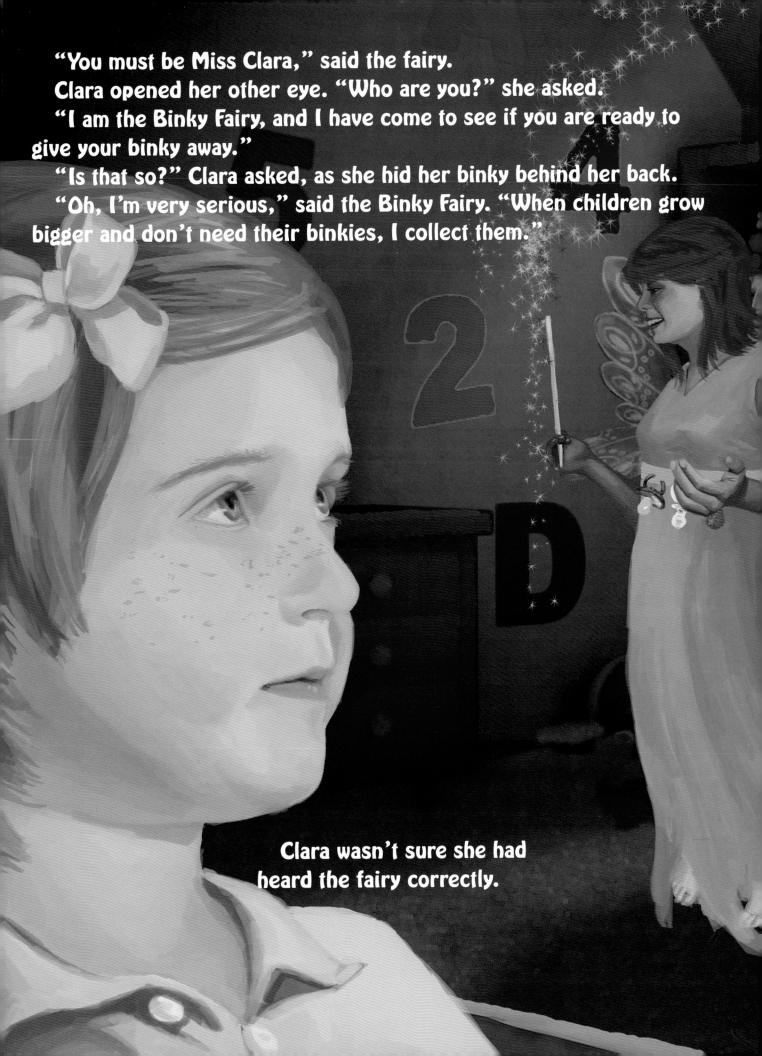

"You must be Miss Clara," said the fairy.
Clara opened her other eye. "Who are you?" she asked.
"I am the Binky Fairy, and I have come to see if you are ready to give your binky away."
"Is that so?" Clara asked, as she hid her binky behind her back.
"Oh, I'm very serious," said the Binky Fairy. "When children grow bigger and don't need their binkies, I collect them."

Clara wasn't sure she had
heard the fairy correctly.

The Binky Fairy fluttered around Clara's room and stopped at the tea party table. A piece of golden saffron cake sat by the tea cup, and Clara could tell the Binky Fairy wanted it.

"Would you like some cake?" asked Clara. "Mommy and I made it."

The fairy giggled. "Thank you. You're very generous."

The Binky Fairy took a tiny bite. Clara felt good about sharing her cake, but she was not ready to share her binky with anyone. So Clara changed the subject.

"What do fairies do in Fairy Land?" Clara asked.

"Oh, we dance and sing and flutter...and we do good deeds."

"What kind of good deeds?" Clara questioned.

"Well, you've heard of the Tooth Fairy, haven't you? She collects baby teeth from under pillows and makes fairy dust with them. Then she sprinkles the dust for happiness and joy."

"The forest fairies take care of the flowers and animals. They scatter dew over the grass, and they call the snails out of their shells in the morning. Some of my best friends are forest fairies."

"Is that so!" stated Clara.

Clara stepped back, startled. "You do what with binkies?"
"All new babies need binkies," said the fairy.
"Why?" asked Clara.
"Because binkies stop babies from crying and help them sleep," replied the fairy.

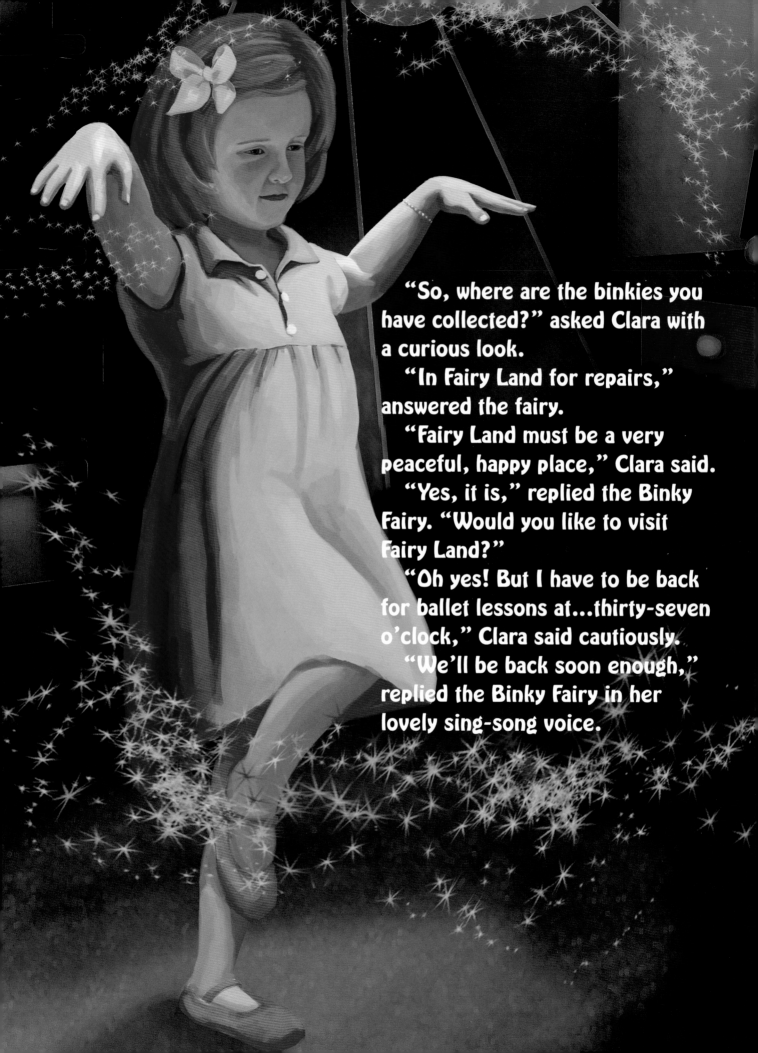

"So, where are the binkies you have collected?" asked Clara with a curious look.

"In Fairy Land for repairs," answered the fairy.

"Fairy Land must be a very peaceful, happy place," Clara said.

"Yes, it is," replied the Binky Fairy. "Would you like to visit Fairy Land?"

"Oh yes! But I have to be back for ballet lessons at...thirty-seven o'clock," Clara said cautiously.

"We'll be back soon enough," replied the Binky Fairy in her lovely sing-song voice.

"Then I'll go!" Clara announced bravely. "I have always wanted to visit Fairy Land. How will we get there?"

"Just close your eyes; hold on to your binky; and think generous thoughts."

"This is the most beautiful place I have ever seen!" said Clara.

The Binky Fairy set Clara down near a brilliant collection of binkies. There were red ones and blue ones and even chartreuse ones. Some were tiny, some were fat, some were rounded, and some were flat; but to Clara, they all sparkled radiantly.

"There are so many, and they are all so 'spectaculicious!'" swooned Clara.

"If I had that many binkies, I would never have to go looking under the sofa, or under my bed, or in drawers again."

"Oh, we usually have many more binkies. Our supply is low right now," said the fairy. "I am afraid we will run out very soon. Do you know how many babies are scheduled to be born this week? One mother will get three all by herself!"

"Well, you can't blame me for the baby boom," Clara announced.

"I know, dear, but I was hoping you would give a generous donation to the Binky fund."

All Clara's life, she had been told that being generous was a good thing. She had learned to share her tea cakes, her dress-up costumes, and even her Monkey Prince, but this was going too far. What was this fairy lady thinking?

Just as Clara was going to say that she didn't
see why she had to donate her binky, the
Binky Fairy led her to a magic reflecting pool
surrounded by beautiful smiling tulips.

"Clara, look into the magic pool," said the
Binky Fairy.

When Clara bent over and looked, she could see a row of crying babies. They were very loud, and they did break her heart, just a little.

"Why are they crying?"
asked Clara.
"Nobody knows for
sure, but they are going
to need all the binkies we
can collect," declared the
Binky Fairy.
"Is that so!" said Clara.

Clara was silent. Then the Binky Fairy told Clara to look into the magic pool again. This time she saw Mommy and Daddy talking to the orthodontist.

"I bet Mommy and Daddy would like me to get rid of my binky too," she thought. "They worry it will make my teeth crooked."

"Look again!" said the Binky Fairy. Unexpectedly, this time Clara could see shelves and shelves of beautiful toys. "How very delightful!" said Clara.

There were soccer balls and robots and teddy bears. And there was something even more spectacular than all the binkies put together. It was a beautiful fairy princess doll with red hair, just like Clara—a grown-up doll, not meant for babies with binkies.

"Who do these toys belong to?"
questioned Clara.

"It's my duty—my fairy duty—to find homes
for all these toys," the Binky Fairy answered.

Clara raised her hand. "I can help with that."

"Perhaps you can. These toys are going to
all the generous boys and girls who are ready
to trade in their binkies," said the Binky Fairy.

"Does my mommy know this plan? I might
want to trade for that beautiful fairy princess
doll with the red hair, when I'm ready," said
Clara quietly.

"I thought so. That doll is very popular.
Perhaps you should do it soon," answered the
Binky Fairy.

Clara had a lot to think about. By now it was almost time for ballet. And Clara felt just a little out of place in Fairy Land because she couldn't flutter.

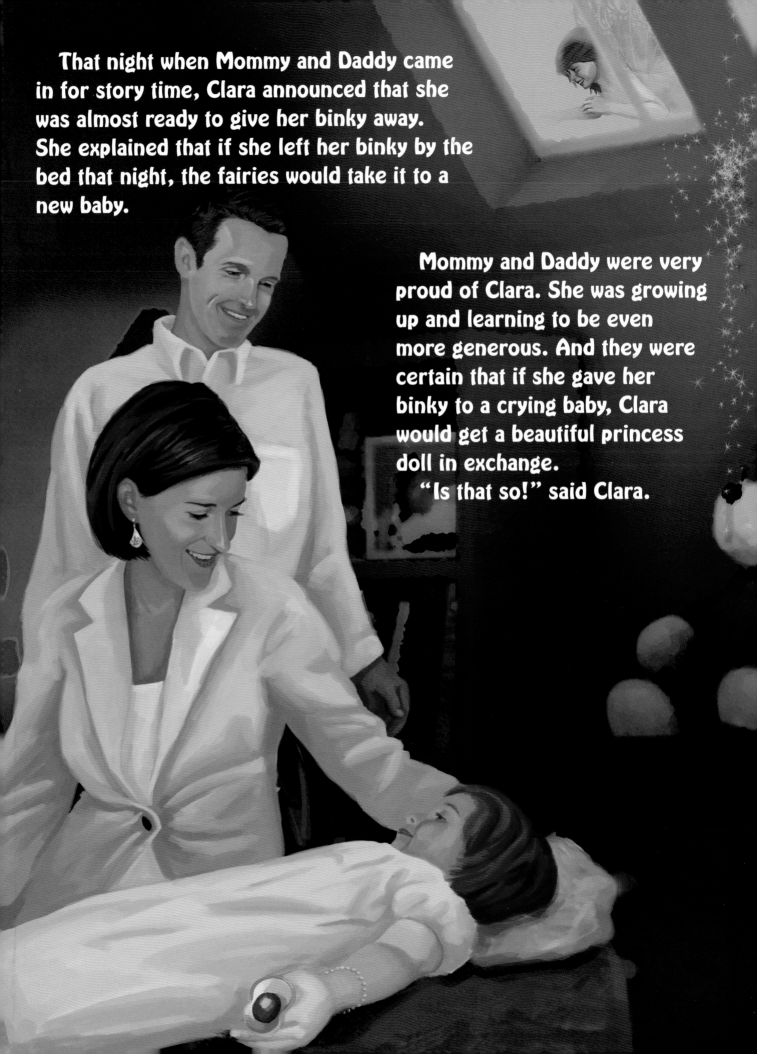

That night when Mommy and Daddy came in for story time, Clara announced that she was almost ready to give her binky away. She explained that if she left her binky by the bed that night, the fairies would take it to a new baby.

Mommy and Daddy were very proud of Clara. She was growing up and learning to be even more generous. And they were certain that if she gave her binky to a crying baby, Clara would get a beautiful princess doll in exchange.

"Is that so!" said Clara.